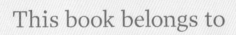

This book belongs to

....

MURILLA GORILLA

JUNGLE DETECTIVE

JENNIFER LLOYD

ILLUSTRATED BY JACQUI LEE

SIMPLY READ BOOKS

To Steve and Carolyn, with whom I shared many happy childhood adventures. —JL

Published in 2013 by Simply Read Books
www.simplyreadbooks.com

Text © 2013 Jennifer Lloyd
Illustrations © 2013 Jacqui Lee

Library and Archives Canada Cataloguing in Publication
Lloyd, Jennifer
Murilla gorilla / by Jennifer Lloyd;
and illustrated by Jacqui Lee.

ISBN 978-1-927018-15-6

Lee, Jacqui II. Title.

PS8623.L69M87 2012   jC813'.6   C2012-903682-X

We gratefully acknowledge for their financial support of our publishing program the Canada Council for the Arts, the BC Arts Council, and the Government of Canada through the Canada Book Fund (CBF).

Manufactured in Malaysia

Book design by Naomi MacDougall

10 9 8 7 6 5 4 3 2

Contents

Chapter 1
Murilla Gets a Case

The bright sun shone over
the African Rainforest.

Murilla Gorilla lived in a hut
on the mountain. She was asleep.

"RING!"

It was her phone.

"Murilla Gorilla Detective
Agency," Murilla said sleepily.

"Murilla, come to Mango Market!
I have a case for you," said
Ms. Chimpanzee.

"Okay," said Murilla.
She hung up the phone.

But Murilla never rushed.

"Zzzz." She went back to sleep.

"RING!"

"Murilla! Where are you?" cried Ms. Chimpanzee.

"I am coming," said Murilla.

Murilla got up slowly.

She looked for her
detective badge.

Murilla's hut was messy.

She found her badge.

It was in the bathtub!

"Now I need my backpack.
Where is it?"

Finally she found it in the fridge.

PUTT! PUTT! Murilla
drove down the mountain.

She always drove very
slowly.

At last, Murilla pulled into
Mango Market.

MANGO MARKET
NEXT LEFT

FRESH FRUIT

11

BROOMS
MOPS

Magnificent
Muffins

CLOSED

AM

1.5/○   '/○

12

Chapter 2
Missing Muffins

Ms. Chimpanzee was at her stall, Magnificent Muffins.

She looked upset.

"What happened?" asked Murilla.

"I made banana muffins today to sell. But someone took them!"

"What did they look like?" asked Murilla.

"Like muffins, of course!"

Murilla drew a picture of muffins in her notebook.

"Where were you when they went missing?" asked Murilla.

"I was looking at Parrot's new parasols. I put Little Chimp in charge."

"Maybe Little Chimp knows who took them," said Murilla.

"Little Chimp?"

No one answered.

Murilla checked for Little Chimp around Ms. Chimpanzee's stall.

She did not see Little Chimp but she saw some small yellow things.

"I need my magnifying glass."

Murilla opened her backpack.

She pulled out two socks,
two shoes and two lollipops.
She pulled out a racket and a birdie.

Ms. Chimpanzee sighed.

At last Murilla pulled out
what she needed.

The small yellow things looked
bigger through the magnifying glass.

"Crumbs!"

Murilla ate them.

"Mmm. They taste like muffins!"

She drew a picture of crumbs in
her notebook.

Chapter 3
The Wrong Tracks

Murilla used her magnifying glass again.

She found some footprints near the crumbs.

"These must belong to the muffin thief!" said Murilla.

Murilla drew a picture of the footprints in her notebook.

Mandrill saw Murilla under the stall.

"What are you doing?" she asked.

"I need to check your footprints,"
said Murilla.

Mandrill stepped in the sand.

Murilla checked.

Mandrill's tracks were too big.

Hippo came by. She stomped
in the sand.

Her tracks were even bigger!

Tree Frog hopped in the sand.

His footprints were too tiny.

"This case is hard work," said Murilla.
"It is time for a break."

She headed to Leopard's Lemonade Stand.

24

Chapter 4
Who Likes Bananas?

"Did you solve the case yet?"
asked Ms. Chimpanzee.

"No. I am still working on it,"
said Murilla. "What were the
muffins made of?"

"BANANAS!" huffed Ms. Chimpanzee.

"Do you like bananas?" asked Murilla.

"Yes," said Ms. Chimpanzee.

Murilla started to draw
Ms. Chimpanzee in her notebook.

"Murilla! I am not the muffin thief!"

"Right! I will ask someone else."

Murilla walked to Anteater's stall.

"What do you like to eat?"
Murilla asked.

"Ants," he said. "Would you like
to buy a crunchy cookie?"

"No thanks," said Murilla.

Murilla walked to Okapi's stall.

"What do you like to eat?"
Murilla asked Okapi.

"Leaves," said Okapi.

Murilla sighed.

OKAPI'S
HAMMOCKS

"This will take a long time,"
said Murilla. "I have a better idea.
I need a disguise."

Murilla looked through her
backpack.

She pulled out her fire hydrant
disguise.

"No. Not that one!"

She pulled out her mailbox
disguise.

"No. Not that one!"

At last she found the perfect one.

Murilla put it on.

She stood very still. She waited.

Soon she heard footsteps. The footsteps got louder and louder.

"This person must love bananas! This must be the muffin thief!"

Chapter 5
Plop!

It was only Ms. Chimpanzee.

"What are you doing?"
she asked Murilla.

"Shh! I am working."

Ms. Chimpanzee rolled her
eyes and left.

Murilla waited. And waited.
And waited.

The sun was hot. The disguise
was hot.

"Time for a nap," Murilla said.
"Zzzz."

PLOP!

Something fell on her head.

It was soft. It was squishy.
Murilla brushed it away.

She went back to sleep.

PLOP!

This time Murilla opened
her eyes.

"A banana peel?"

Murilla looked up. She saw
Little Chimp!

"Little Chimp come down here!"

Little Chimp climbed higher.

Murilla took off her banana tree disguise. She flashed her detective badge.

Finally Little Chimp climbed down.

Murilla checked his feet.

His tracks were a perfect match.

"Did you eat the muffins?"

Little Chimp looked away.
He said nothing.

"Little Chimp, tell the truth!"

"Yes, I ate them. I am sorry."

That afternoon, Little Chimp
helped Ms. Chimpanzee make a
new batch of banana muffins.

They wanted to give one to
Murilla, but....

Murilla was fast asleep.

"Zzzz."